Dear Parent:
Your child's love of reading starts here!

Every child learns to read in a different way and at his or her own speed. Some go back and forth between reading levels and read favorite books again and again. Others read through each level in order. You can help your young reader improve and become more confident by encouraging his or her own interests and abilities. From books your child reads with you to the first books he or she reads alone, there are I Can Read Books for every stage of reading:

SHARED READING
Basic language, word repetition, and whimsical illustrations, ideal for sharing with your emergent reader

BEGINNING READING
Short sentences, familiar words, and simple concepts for children eager to read on their own

READING WITH HELP
Engaging stories, longer sentences, and language play for developing readers

READING ALONE
Complex plots, challenging vocabulary, and high-interest topics for the independent reader

ADVANCED READING
Short paragraphs, chapters, and exciting themes for the perfect bridge to chapter books

I Can Read Books have introduced children to the joy of reading since 1957. Featuring award-winning authors and illustrators and a fabulous cast of beloved characters, I Can Read Books set the standard for beginning readers.

A lifetime of discovery begins with the magical words "I Can Read!"

Visit www.icanread.com for information
on enriching your child's reading experience.

For Thompson Daniel and Anna Aurelia
—A.S.C.

Library of Congress Cataloging-in-Publication Data
Capucilli, Alyssa Satin.
  Biscuit and the baby / story by Alyssa Satin Capucilli ; pictures by Pat Schories.
    p.   cm.—(A my first I can read book)
  Summary: Biscuit, a young puppy, is eager to meet the new baby but must wait until nap time is over.
  ISBN-10: 0-06-009459-1 (trade bdg.) — ISBN-13: 978-0-06-009459-1 (trade bdg.)
  ISBN-10: 0-06-009460-5 (lib. bdg.) — ISBN-13: 978-0-06-009460-7 (lib. bdg.)
  ISBN-10: 0-06-009461-3 (pbk.) — ISBN-13: 978-0-06-009461-4 (pbk.)
  [1. Dogs—Fiction. 2. Babies—Fiction.] I. Schories, Pat, ill. II. Title. III. Series.
PZ7.C179Bie 2005   2003025271
[E]—dc22   CIP
                                                                                               AC

❖

09 10 11 12 13 SCP 10 9 8 7 6 5

I Can Read!

SHARED
My
First
READING

Biscuit
and the Baby

story by ALYSSA SATIN CAPUCILLI
pictures by PAT SCHORIES

HarperCollins*Publishers*

Woof, woof!
What does Biscuit see?

Woof, woof!

Biscuit sees the baby.

Biscuit wants
to meet the baby!

Woof, woof!

Sshhh! Quiet, Biscuit.

The baby is sleeping.

It's not time
to meet the baby yet.

Woof, woof!

Biscuit sees the baby's rattle.

Woof, woof!

Biscuit sees the baby's bunny.

Woof, woof!
Biscuit wants
to meet the baby!

Sshhh! Quiet, Biscuit.
The baby is still sleeping.
It's not time
to meet the baby yet.

Woof, woof!

Silly puppy!

That's not your blanket.

Oh no, Biscuit.
Those booties
are for the baby.
Woof, woof!

Funny puppy!

You want to meet the baby.

But it's not time

to meet the baby yet.

Woof!

Waa! Waa! Waa! Waa!

18

Woof! Woof! Woof! Woof!

Biscuit, come back.

It's only the baby!

Woof, woof!

Here, sweet puppy.
Now it's time
to meet the baby.
Woof, woof!

Best of all, it's time
for the baby to meet
a new friend!

Woof!

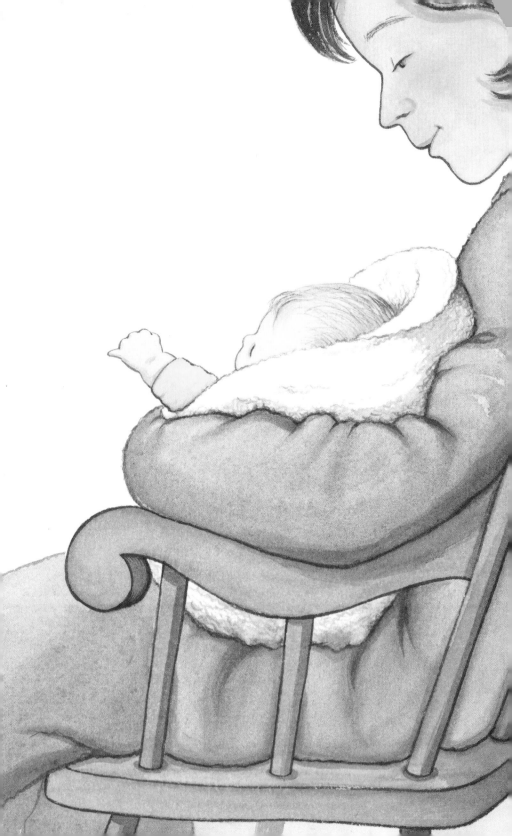